A Molly Book

MOLLY

By Joseph S. Bonsall

Illustrated by Erin Marie Mauterer

Ideals Children's Books • Nashville, Tennessee
an imprint of Hambleton-Hill Publishing, Inc.

To my lovely wife, Mary, who taught me all about cats and their love. To Pumpkin, Omaha, Gypsy, and wonderful Molly, for all my inspiration. To Spooker, for stopping by the Home. And to Yuri—if only we all had his spirit. Rest well in The Better Place, little gray friend.

—J. S. B.

Dedicated to the cat's meow—Mona, Max, Dart, Joeii, Taz, Lance, and Bradley. How you stir my heart!

—E. M. M.

Text copyright © 1997 by Joseph S. Bonsall
Illustrations copyright © 1997 by Hambleton-Hill Publishing, Inc.

Published by Ideals Children's Books
An imprint of Hambleton-Hill Publishing, Inc.
Nashville, Tennessee 37218

Printed and bound in Mexico

Library of Congress Cataloging-in-Publication Data
Bonsall, Joseph S.
    Molly / by Joseph Bonsall ; illustrated by Erin Marie Mauterer. —
1st ed.
        p.   cm. — (A Molly book)
    Summary: An orphaned calico cat dreams of how, as a kitten, she
came to live with Mother Mary and her three feline companions.
    ISBN 1-57102-122-1 (hc)
    [1. Cats—Fiction. 2. Orphans—Fiction.] I. Mauterer, Erin,
ill. II. Title. III. Series: Bonsall, Joseph S. Molly book.
PZ7.B64275Mo   1997
[E]—DC21   97-10889
                                                                CIP
                                                                AC

The illustrations in this book were rendered in watercolor, gouache, colored
    pencil, and acrylic.
The text type was set in ACaslon Regular.
The display type was set in ACaslon SwashBoldItalic and ACaslon BoldItalic.
Color separations were made by Color 4, Inc.
Printed and bound by R.R. Donnelley & Sons Company.

First Edition

10 9 8 7 6 5 4 3 2 1

The smallest feline is a masterpiece.

—Leonardo da Vinci

Molly was two years old and a fully grown cat, though she still looked somewhat like a kitten. It's just that she never grew very big.

Molly thought that perhaps it had something to do with her beginnings, not that she remembered much about them. But she did recall, and she even sometimes dreamed about, the night that a young humancat picked her up out of the rain and brought her to the Home and to Mother Mary.

Now, as Molly lay napping in her bed, she dreamed once again of that night two years ago.

Molly's dream was quite clear, and in it she was a tiny kitten again. Looking around she could see that she was in a dark, cold place littered with hay and old newspapers. Altogether there were five kittens here, but she was by far the smallest.

Then suddenly there were voices! Loud and terrible voices!

"That darned cat had kittens again!" growled one voice.

"How many this time?" asked another.

"Looks like four."

"What should we do?"

"Well, let's get 'em out from under that porch and put 'em in a box. Then we'll take 'em over to the animal shelter. One mangy, old cat around here is enough!" said the loud, terrible voice.

Then a young male humancat reached under the porch and grabbed four of the kittens by the scruff of the neck. He put them in a box and carried them away. He didn't see the littlest one, and so she was left alone and shivering in the dark.

As Molly dreamed on, she remembered being so-o-o-o scared, so-o-o-o hungry, and so-o-o-o cold!

Then she heard a voice inside her head, calling out in perfect catspeak (which is, of course, the language of cats). It was the mother cat searching for her kittens.

"Oh my! They have taken my children! I just can't believe this! I'll scratch their eyes out . . . I'll make them sorry . . . I'll . . ."

"Mew."

"What?" exclaimed the mother cat, turning toward the sound.

"Meeeow," wailed the little voice in the corner.

"Well, my, my, my, they forgot you, my littlest baby," purred the mother cat softly. Washing her kitten's face, the mother cat sadly realized that she must find a new home for her little one before she too was taken away— even though it would mean losing her kitten forever.

Gently she picked the little one up in her mouth, as mother cats do, and carried her out into the pouring rain.

She walked and walked for what seemed like miles, praying inside her heart that the God of All Creatures would save her little baby.

As they rounded a turn in the road, the mother cat's prayers were answered.

Coming toward them, with his collar turned up against the driving rain, was a familiar young humancat who had been kind to the mother cat many times. He was always warm and friendly, not like the mean ones who lived on the farm.

Seeing him, the mother cat carefully placed her little one by a large oak tree.

Then she hid herself and watched.

"Meeeooowww," cried the little kitten.

"Wh—What? WOW!" exclaimed the young boy, who was named Gabe. "What are you doing out here in the middle of nowhere?" He scooped up the cold, wet kitten and cradled her inside his warm coat.

"I've gotta get you warmed up and dried off. I'll bet you're really hungry too!" the boy said as he hurried down the road, gently carrying the last and the smallest of the mother cat's litter.

The mother cat watched as Gabe disappeared down the road. Then she turned and slowly began the long journey back to the farm. Her heart was heavy with sadness, though she knew she had done the right thing.

Silently she prayed to the God of All Creatures, who most certainly watched over all kitties, and asked him to find a good home for her baby.

Farther down the road, young Gabe walked up a long driveway and knocked on the door. The tiny treasure that he carried would soon change the lives of all who lived in the house.

"Oh, Gabe," said his Aunt Mary, who opened the door, "just look at her, so small and wet. I'll bet she's only about six weeks old. And, oh my, look at those colors. She's a calico, all right. Wherever did you find her?"

"I was just on my way home, Aunt Mary, and there she was, under the old oak tree by McNichols' Pond," Gabe explained. "I knew my mom wouldn't let me keep her, so I thought I'd bring her to you."

Mary held the little tyke in her arms and softly whispered, "You're home now, sweet kitty. There's no need for you to worry anymore. I think I'll call you . . . Molly."

Molly didn't understand a word of the human's catspeak. She was so young that she barely understood her own language. But she did know that she was safe and warm, and that she was *home* with Mother Mary.

Mother Mary gently dried Molly's colorful fur with a hair dryer. (Molly was not entirely happy about that.)

Then the wonderful humancat gave Molly some food. (Molly was *very* happy about that.)

Taking Molly up a long flight of stairs, Mother Mary went into one of the rooms. She placed the kitten on a warm blanket. Then closing the door quietly behind her, she left Molly alone so that she could get used to her new surroundings.

After a little while, Molly thought she could hear other cats talking outside the door. She couldn't quite make out what they were saying, but she understood enough to know that they were talking about her.

"Oh boy, just what we need around here—another cat!" grumbled Gypsy, her half-mustache twitching slightly under her nose.

"Now, don't get yourself in an uproar," answered a big, orange cat named Pumpkin. "Mother Mary always knows best."

Omaha purred, "I think she's beautiful!"

Just then, Mother Mary came back down the hall. Seeing that the three cats were curious about the newcomer, she opened the door and let them in to meet Molly.

Molly, a little frightened, stared at the three cats, and they stared back.

"Okay now, Molly," whispered Mother Mary softly, "this big, orange fellow is Pumpkin. He's the oldest of the crowd. This handsome little gray and white kitty is named Omaha, and this big girl is Gypsy.

"Now you three make Molly feel at home, because she's going to be living with us from now on."

After Mother Mary left, the three cats gathered around the tiny kitten.

"Hi there," purred Omaha in his friendliest catspeak. Then he asked, "Hey, Pumpkin, why does her tail have that little curl on the end?"

Pumpkin, who was not only the oldest but also the wisest of the three cats, thought a moment and then answered, "It is said that a cat whose tail has that enchanted little curl on the end is a cat who has been specially blessed by the God of All Creatures."

"Wow," said Omaha. He already adored little Molly.

"Ah, what a bunch of cat litter!" huffed Gypsy. "I will just warn you right now, stay away from my things. That includes *my* toys, *my* bowl, and *any* spot that I choose to lie upon." Gypsy then turned and strutted right out of the room.

"Umm . . . ahh . . . what is . . . uh . . . her problem?" purred Molly in soft, broken catspeak.

Molly's first spoken words made Pumpkin and Omaha burst right out laughing. Little Molly laughed right along with them.

Molly's first day at the Home was quite an adventure. There was no end to the places that needed exploring. By the end of the day, Molly had decided that she loved her new home and her new friends—wise old Pumpkin, sweet little Omaha, and even grouchy Gypsy.

And how the little lost kitten loved Mother Mary. This wonderful humancat filled the kitten's heart with warmth. Molly was safe and warm and dry, just as her mother had prayed she would be. As Pumpkin had said, Molly was truly blessed.

Molly woke up from her dreams and found herself in her warm bed. As she thought about how she had come to the Home, she said a quiet prayer, thanking the God of All Creatures for answering her mother's prayers those two years ago.

Molly thought that she just had to be the happiest little cat in the whole wide world.